CAPTAIN SNOUT
AND THE SUPER POWER QUESTIONS

PRESENTED TO:

_____

WITH LOVE FROM:

_____

To Eli, Emmy, Liam and Louie.
Stop the ANTs!
–DA

For Katie and Chris.
–BK

ZONDERKIDZ

Captain Snout and the Super Power Questions
Copyright © 2017 by Dr. Daniel Amen
Illustrations © 2017 by Brendan Kearney

Requests for information should be addressed to:

Zonderkidz, 3900 Sparks Drive SE, Grand Rapids, Michigan 49546

ISBN 978-0-310-75832-7

Any Internet addresses (websites, blogs, etc.) and telephone numbers in this book are offered as a resource. They are not intended in any way to be or imply an endorsement by Zondervan, nor does Zondervan vouch for the content of these sites and numbers for the life of this book.

All rights reserved. No part of this publication may be reproduced, stored in a retrieval system, or transmitted in any form or by any means—electronic, mechanical, photocopy, recording, or any other—except for brief quotations in printed reviews, without the prior permission of the publisher.

Zonderkidz is a trademark of Zondervan.

Contributor: *Jill Gorey*
Art direction: *Ron Huizinga*

Printed in China

21 /DSC/ 20 19 18 17 16 15 14 13 12 11 10 9 8 7 6

The Pennypepper children
wanted a puppy more than anything.

Their parents said,
"YES!"

... but not until the kids
earned enough money to
buy some of the supplies
their new furry friend
would need.

So the children decided to have a car wash. Sam made a sign.
Annabelle brought out the hose, buckets, and sponges.
And Chloe made some soapy water.

Washing cars was FUN, and everyone felt
HAPPY and HOPEFUL and EXCITED . . .

until the customers stopped coming.

It's all YOUR fault!

Now we'll NEVER get our puppy!

THIS IS THE **WORST** CAR WASH EVER!

Everyone was feeling **BAD.**

Sam was sad, Chloe was mad, and Annabelle was worried and upset! Their unhappy thoughts made them want to give up.

But then help arrived.

I AM CAPTAIN SNOUT!

"And I have come to save you from all of those horrible and unhappy thoughts!"

"What do you mean?" the children asked.

"THOUGHTS HAVE POWER!"

the superhero announced.
"They can change how you feel! They can make you feel GOOD, or they can make you feel ROTTEN!"

"We feel rotten, all right," said the Pennypeppers.

"And no wonder! Your heads are filled with ANTs—

AUTOMATIC NEGATIVE THOUGHTS."

"ANTs are thoughts that pop into your mind uninvited.
They make you feel:

MAD, SAD, WORRIED, OR UPSET

And most of the time they're
NOT EVEN TRUE!"

"I don't want ANTs!" Chloe cried.

"No need to fear!"
said Captain Snout.

Captain Snout explained how the Super Power Questions worked.

"Sam, you said NO ONE wants you to wash their car. Now watch my Super Power Questions challenge that thought."

IS THAT TRUE? ARE YOU 100% SURE NO ONE WANTS YOU TO WASH THEIR CAR?

"We already had some customers," Sam admitted.

"And there could be more," said Chloe.

The Pennypeppers realized their negative thoughts weren't necessarily true. And these new thoughts made them feel much better!

You see? Super Power Questions can help your brain think better! And they can defeat all kinds of ANTs!

Let me show you how...

These sneaky ANTs steal your happiness! They hang around with unhappy thoughts that make you feel sorry for yourself. They don't use words like "sometimes" or "maybe".

All-or-Nothing ANTs say things like:

ALL of the cars just drive by!

We will NEVER make any money!

There's NOTHING we can do!

When an ALL-or-NOTHING ANT
sneaks in, send it
PACKING!

This ANT can't see anything good! Its beady eyes ZOOM in on mistakes and problems and fill your head with negative thoughts like:

Today is a BAD day!

My sign looks TERRIBLE.

This is the WORST car wash EVER!

Maybe if no one showed up at all.

Or it was snowing.

Or a monster ate all the cars!

THERE YOU GO! Look at that ANT skedaddle!

Don't listen to this lying ANT!
The Fortune Teller ANT thinks it can see what is
going to happen in the future, but all it
really does is think up bad stuff like:

We'll **NEVER**
make any money.

We'll **NEVER**
get our puppy.

The Mind Reader ANT thinks it can see inside someone else's mind. It thinks it knows how others THINK and FEEL without EVEN BEING TOLD!

It says things like:

EVERYBODY thinks we'll do a BAD job!

They are all LAUGHING at us.

"Of course, it's not true!" Sam exclaimed.
"We DON'T know what others are thinking. Let's blast this ANT!"

The BLAMING ANT

When things go wrong,
the Blaming ANT always
sings the same old sad song:

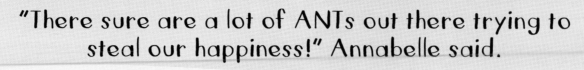

"There sure are a lot of ANTs out there trying to steal our happiness!" Annabelle said.

"Don't let them!" Captain Snout replied. "The next time those negative thoughts pop into your head, ask the Super Power Questions."

IS THAT TRUE? ARE YOU 100% SURE IT'S TRUE?

The children thanked their superhero
for saving them from their
SAD, MAD, and
UNHAPPY thoughts.

"I see my job here is done,"
said Captain Snout.

"But yours has just *BEGUN!*"

With no ANTs making them feel bad, the Pennypeppers were excited to get back to work.

THE BEST
CAR WASH
EVER!

They spruced up their sign and added some
brightly colored balloons.
Before long, there was a BIG line of FRIENDS
and NEIGHBORS waiting for a wash.

Thanks to Captain Snout and those Super Power Questions,
the Pennypeppers had TRUER and HAPPIER thoughts.

They earned enough money to buy toys and supplies for Zeus,
their new puppy . . . and he was the perfect addition to the family.